Hello, Family Members,

Learning to read is one of the most important accomplishments of early childhood. **Hello Reader!** books are designed to help children become skilled readers who like to read. Beginning readers learn to read by remembering frequently used words like "the," "is," and "and"; by using phonics skills to decode new words; and by interpreting picture and text clues. These books provide both the stories children enjoy and the structure they need to read fluently and independently. Here are suggestions for helping your child *before, during,* and *after* reading:

Before

• Look at the cover and pictures and have your child predict what the story is about.
• Read the story to your child.
• Encourage your child to chime in with familiar words and phrases.
• Echo read with your child by reading a line first and having your child read it after you do.

During

• Have your child think about a word he or she does not recognize right away. Provide hints such as "Let's see if we know the sounds" and "Have we read other words like this one?"
• Encourage your child to use phonics skills to sound out new words.
• Provide the word for your child when more assistance is needed so that he or she does not struggle and the experience of reading with you is a positive one.
• Encourage your child to have fun by reading with a lot of expression . . . like an actor!

After

• Have your child keep lists of interesting and favorite words.
• Encourage your child to read the books over and over again. Have him or her read to brothers, sisters, grandparents, and even teddy bears. Repeated readings develop confidence in young readers.
• Talk about the stories. Ask and answer questions. Share ideas about the funniest and most interesting characters and events in the stories.

I do hope that you and your child enjoy this book.

—Francie Alexander
    Reading Specialist,
    Scholastic's Instructional Publishing Group

If you have questions or comments about how children learn to read, please contact Francie Alexander at FrancieAl@aol.com

To Grace, Gina, and Kimberly —
great parents to this book
— E.L.

For my parents, with love
— D.B.

Text copyright © 1998 by Elizabeth Levy.
Illustrations copyright © 1998 by Denise Brunkus.
All rights reserved. Published by Scholastic Inc.
HELLO READER! and CARTWHEEL BOOKS and associated logos
are trademarks and/or registered trademarks of Scholastic Inc.

Library of Congress Cataloging-in-Publication Data
Levy, Elizabeth.
    Parents' night fright / by Elizabeth Levy; illustrated by Denise Brunkus.
        p.   cm. — (Invisible Inc.; #6)   (Hello reader! Level 4)
    "Cartwheel books."
    Summary: Charlene's story is voted best in the class, but when she goes to read it at Parents' Night, it has vanished from her folder.
    ISBN 0-590-60324-8
    [1. Schools — Fiction.   2. Mystery and detective stories.]
    I. Brunkus, Denise, ill.   II. Title.   III. Series.   IV. Series: Levy, Elizabeth.
    Invisible Inc.; #6.
PZ7.L5827Par   1998   97-14294
[Fic] — dc21   CIP
                                                                      AC

10 9 8 7 6 5 4 3 2 1   8 9/9 0/0 01 02

Printed in the U.S.A.   24
First printing, March 1998

NVISIBLE INC. #6

Parents' Night Fright

by Elizabeth Levy

Illustrated by
Denise Brunkus

Hello Reader! — Level 4

SCHOLASTIC INC. Cartwheel
·B·O·O·K·S·®
New York Toronto London Auckland Sydney

Chip fell into a strange pool of water. Now Chip is invisible!
Justin knows how to read lips because of his hearing loss.
Charlene is sometimes bossy but always brave.
Together they are **Invisible Inc.** — *and they solve mysteries!*

CHAPTER 1

Master of Doom

Charlene raced out the door as the bell rang for the end of school. She hadn't been in such a good mood in ages.

"I won! I won!" she shouted to Chip and Justin. "Can you believe it? My story got picked to be read aloud on Parents' Night."

"You deserve it!" said Justin. "Your story really was the best."

"Now maybe my parents will stop talking about my 'genius' brother, Philip," said Charlene as she joyfully kicked at some pebbles on the sidewalk. "Wow! I can't believe I won!"

"Charlene," said Pamela, a new girl at school, "it's in very poor taste to brag. Personally, I thought Chip's story on the problems of being invisible was touching." She turned toward Chip. "The fact that you see people stare at you, but they can't see you stare back — that moved me."

"But Charlene's was still the funniest story," said Chip.

Pamela made a face. It annoyed
her that Chip and Justin were
actually happy for Charlene. But
that's what happens when you're
partners. Chip, Charlene, and
Justin ran Invisible Inc. They solved
mysteries. And when one of them
got good news, the others were
always happy, too.

Pamela turned to Justin. She spoke slowly and very loudly. "JUSTIN — it's so AMAZING that you can READ my lips and UNDERSTAND everything I SAY!"

"That's because you have such a big mouth," said Charlene. Chip and Justin laughed.

"You know," Pamela said in a snobby voice, "insults are a very inferior form of humor." She swung her long, dark hair and strolled away.

"I'm sorry," Charlene called after her. She knew Pamela was right about insults, but being nice to the new teacher's pet wasn't easy for Charlene.

Just then a boy raced by on a bicycle. He was wearing a black cape with red trim.

"Make way, make way!" he
shouted. "The Master of Doom is
upon you!"

Like Pamela, Paul Jacoby was
new to the school. But unlike
Pamela, he was a lot more fun.

Paul loved horror stories and liked to dress up like Count Dracula. The teachers were getting a little tired of his costumes, but the kids in Invisible Inc. thought he was cool.

Paul slowed his bike and waved. "Beware!" he shouted. "Parents' Night could be a terrible fright!"

Justin and Chip laughed as Paul sped away, but Charlene looked worried.

"You don't really think anything bad will happen on Parents' Night, do you?" she asked with a frown.

"No way," said Chip. "Paul's just talking. This Parents' Night is going to be great — even better than your brother Philip's."

"Speaking of Philip — there he is," said Justin.

Charlene's older brother skated
by with a group of friends from
junior high. Philip rarely had
anything to do with Charlene and
her friends from elementary school
— especially the detectives from
Invisible Inc.

"Hey, Philip!" shouted Charlene. "We had a story contest. Guess who everybody voted for to read her story on Parents' Night!"

"It's 'guess *whom*,' " said Philip. "How could you have won when you can't even speak correctly?"

Charlene looked like a balloon that had lost all of its air.

"Will you proofread it for me?" she asked in a tiny voice.

"Maybe," Philip said, looking annoyed. "But only if I have time." He flung his scarf over his shoulder, nearly hitting Chip in the head with the black-and-red fringes.

"What's wrong with Philip these days?" asked Justin as he watched Charlene's brother skate away.

"My mom and dad are worried about him," said Charlene. "His teacher called them in for a conference. There are a lot of smart kids in junior high and Philip's not the smartest anymore." Charlene tried not to look too happy.

"Well, wait till your parents hear that you're the best writer in the class," said Justin.

"I never do anything as well as Philip," said Charlene softly.

"You will on Parents' Night!" said Chip. "Just wait and see. It's going to be the best Parents' Night that ever was!"

CHAPTER 2

It's Not an Award Ceremony

On Parents' Night, Charlene came downstairs in black tights, a black skirt, and a black turtleneck.

"Do I look like a writer?" she asked.

"You look like a vampire," said Charlene's little brother, Stanley. "You look like that creepy kid in the third grade who wears that cape."

"You could add a little color," suggested Charlene's mother. "Maybe you can borrow Philip's red-and-black scarf."

"No way," said Philip. "She borrows half my clothes already."

"But tonight's important," said Charlene. "Did you proofread my paper?"

"It's in your folder," Philip answered. "I don't know why you're making such a big deal out of this. Parents' Night is nothing."

"You didn't say that when you were in elementary school and won the science prize every year," said Charlene's mother.

"This is my very first Parents' Night," said Stanley. "Mom and Dad are going to spend the whole time in my class."

"No, they're not, dodo-head," said Charlene. "They're going to hear my story. Everybody voted mine the best."

"I just wish everybody would leave," Philip said, putting his hands over his ears. "I have homework to do!" Philip had just started to stay home by himself without a baby-sitter.

Charlene's mom kissed Philip good-bye. "I remember your first Parents' Night when you were in kindergarten," she said to him. "The teacher had your work all over the room."

"*My* work is all over *my* classroom," bragged Stanley.

Charlene sighed. It wasn't easy having Philip as an older brother and Stanley as a younger brother. She felt squashed in between.

* * *

At the school that night, everyone
greeted each other on the front
steps. Many of the parents stared at
Chip. The students had gotten used
to him, but an invisible kid still
shocked a lot of adults.

As usual, Paul was wearing his
cape. His mother had on an
identical cape and was dressed
all in black.

"I hear she writes comedy for TV," said Justin's mother.

"I told you writers wear black," said Charlene to her mother.

Outside Mr. Gonshak's classroom, Pamela was sitting at a desk in the hall.

"The teacher asked me to be on hall duty," she said. "Put your folders right here. That way parents can look through your work while they're going between classes."

"Have you ever heard anybody so bossy?" whispered Charlene as she put down her folder. Chip and Justin laughed.

Mr. Gonshak invited all the children and their parents into the classroom. Keith Broder and his parents arrived a little late. As Keith put his folder down on the table,

Pamela leaned over and said something to him. Justin frowned as he watched her from inside the room.

Mr. Gonshak asked everyone to take a seat.

"Welcome, parents," he said. "I want to begin by telling you how proud I am of my class this year. I don't think I've ever had a finer crop of writers."

Mr. Gonshak smiled at Charlene as he continued.

"Now I'd like you all to hear the story our class voted to be read to you. Pamela, will you please bring up Charlene's writing portfolio?"

Charlene went to the front of the room. "I'd like to thank the many people who helped me," she said. "My best friends, Chip and Justin, who read my story and encouraged me ... my parents ... "

Pamela handed Charlene her folder. "It's not an award ceremony," she said.

Keith Broder laughed. Charlene blushed as she opened her folder. Suddenly, her eyes widened in horror.

"Is something wrong?" asked Mr. Gonshak.

"It's not here," said Charlene. Charlene's story wasn't in her folder. In its place was a blank piece of paper. "My story is gone!"

Mr. Gonshak tried to calm Charlene down. "Maybe you dropped it in the hall. Why don't we all take a walk to the cafeteria for refreshments? Perhaps if Charlene finds her story, she can read it to us at the end of the night."

"Don't worry, Mr. Gonshak," said Justin. "Invisible Inc. is on the case."

CHAPTER 3

A Proper Detective Is Always Prepared

"I've got to tell you what I found out when I lip-read," said Justin excitedly. "I think I know ..."

Before Justin could finish, Pamela interrupted. "I can help you, Charlene," she said. "I feel so bad about your missing paper."

"Well, you should," said Charlene. "You were the hall monitor. And now my paper is gone!"

"I am a very responsible person," said Pamela. "That's why I'm offering to help your silly Invisible Inc. club."

"It's not silly and it's not a club," said Chip. "We're detectives. We right wrongs." Chip handed her one of their cards.

"It's blank," said Pamela.

"Written in invisible ink," said Charlene proudly. "That was my idea. If you hold it up to a lightbulb or something warm, you'll be able to read it."

Pamela put their card in her pocket. "Well, I'm very smart—so I'm sure I'll make an excellent detective."

"Thank you, but we don't need your help," said Justin. "In fact ..."

"Oh, but you do," said Pamela. "I sat at the desk in the hall the whole time. Nobody could have touched your folder while I was on duty."

Charlene looked crushed. "But somebody did!" she cried.

"However," continued Pamela, "I did leave my desk once to run to the water fountain. You know, it's very healthy to drink water. I make sure to drink eight glasses a day."

"Could you get to the point?" asked Chip impatiently. "What happened when you went to get water?"

"Well," said Pamela, "when I got back, I saw something black-and-red flap around the corner. But I'm not sure what it was."

"Paul told us to beware of a
Parents' Night fright," said Chip
excitedly. "He always wears a black-
and-red cape."

"But . . . ," said Justin slowly.

Pamela ignored Justin. She took out a notebook and pen. "A proper detective is always prepared," she said. "Chip, put on your invisible clothes so nobody can see you. Find out where Paul was when the folder was taken. I'll help by questioning some of the other students. We'll meet in twenty minutes in the cafeteria." Pamela snapped shut her notebook and took off.

"Who made her boss?" asked Justin. "She's not part of Invisible Inc."

"She gave us a good clue," said Charlene.

"Let's meet in fifteen minutes, not twenty," said Justin. "And *outside* the cafeteria—not inside."

"Why?" asked Chip.

Justin looked mysterious.
"Let's just say I have my
reasons," he said. "But first, find
out what you can about Paul."

CHAPTER 4
Playing Games

Chip went into the boys' room and changed into his invisible clothes. He looked all over for Paul. The halls were crowded with parents and students.

Slipping past a group of kids, Chip peeked in the gym. Mr. Weinstein, the science teacher, had set up The Body Game. Parents and students were racing up and down a giant paper display of the body that lay on the floor. They were in two teams—red and blue. The first team to make it to the lungs would win.

Chip spotted Paul and his mother talking to the science teacher near the brain. He stood behind them quietly so he could hear what they were saying.

"I'm sorry to keep you so long,"
said Mr. Weinstein to Paul's mother.
"But we have to resolve the issue of
Paul's cape. I'm afraid it's too dan-
gerous for him to wear it in school."

Paul's mother nodded. "Paul,
there are some times that rules
count. I think you should agree not
to wear your cape."

Mr. Weinstein breathed a sigh of
relief.

"Thank you for your cooperation,"
he said, looking at his watch. "I'm
afraid I've taken up all of your time
since you arrived."

"That's all right," Paul's mother answered.

As the science teacher turned to hurry away, a gust of wind rushed past him.

"My," he said to himself, "this gym is getting drafty."

* * *

Justin and Charlene were waiting for Chip outside the cafeteria.

"I don't see how it could be Paul," said Chip. "Mr. Weinstein has been talking to him and his mother ever since Parents' Night began."

"Now what?" groaned Charlene. "Paul was our main suspect."

"I know who took your paper, Charlene," said Justin. "I've known all along."

"You have?" asked Charlene. "Who?"

"Pamela," said Justin. "I tried to tell you before, but she kept interrupting. Just before class, I read her lips when she was talking to Keith Broder."

"What was she saying?" asked Chip.

"Pamela told Keith her paper was better than yours," said Justin. "She said her story should have been voted the best."

"She's the perfect suspect," said Charlene. "She had motive *and* opportunity."

"And besides, she's a real snob," said Chip.

"Let me at her!" cried Charlene. "She's in the cafeteria. I saw her questioning all the parents and teachers."

"We don't need her kind of help," said Justin. "She offered to help only because she didn't want us to suspect her."

The group split up in the cafeteria so that they could find Pamela quickly. Charlene's parents were with Stanley. They waved to Charlene from across the room.

"Did you find your paper?" asked Charlene's father.

Stanley showed Charlene his artwork made out of dried macaroni. "It's a dinosaur," he said proudly.

"I don't have time for macaroni dinosaurs," said Charlene impatiently. "Have you seen that thief Pamela? She stole my paper."

"Pamela?" said Charlene's mom. "She told me that she was helping you and had really liked your paper."

"She lied," sputtered Charlene. "Wait until I find her ..."

"Wait!" cried Justin as he ran up to Charlene. "I have some new information. I might have been wrong." Justin signaled to Chip to meet them outside.

"I talked to Pamela," said Justin. "I told her that I read her lips. She admits she complained to Keith, but she said she voted for Chip. She thought it wasn't in 'good taste' to vote for herself."

"That's so Pamela," said Charlene angrily. She waved her hands in the air, accidentally knocking Chip into the bushes.

"Ouch!" said Chip.

"I'm sorry," Charlene said quickly. "I didn't mean to push you."

"It wasn't your push. Somebody parked a bicycle in this bush," said Chip, rubbing his knee. "What a dumb place to leave a bike!"

Charlene went to help Chip.

"Hey! That's Philip's bike," she said. "What's Philip doing here?"

"You know," said Justin slowly, "I think maybe we've been angry at the wrong person."

CHAPTER 5

Too Tough for Monsters

Invisible Inc. rushed back into school. Philip was standing outside of the gym talking to Mr. Weinstein.

"Philip," gushed Mr. Weinstein, "it's so good to see you again. I'm so happy that one of my star pupils wanted to come back on Parents' Night. You helped me create The Body Game. I bet you could go through the course in record time."

"Star pupil," muttered Charlene. "I'll make him see stars." She ran after Philip, who had already started up the arm of The Body Game. "Give me back my paper!" Charlene yelled.

"Careful!" shouted Chip.

But it was too late. Charlene tripped on something red-and-black

that lay on the gym floor.

"Hey!" shouted Pamela as she entered the gym. "I recognize that." Pamela ran to pick up the scarf. "This is what I saw in the hallway. Now I remember—it had fringes."

"Philip," said Charlene, "you took my paper. You couldn't stand that I did something good."

"Excuse me, Mr. Weinstein," said Philip. "I have to talk to my little sister and her little friends."

Justin, Chip, Charlene, and Philip walked into the hallway. Pamela tagged along.

"You stole my paper," said Charlene. "I asked you to proofread it, but instead you took it!"

"I did proofread it," said Philip with a smug look. "Invisible Inc. just isn't as good at solving mysteries as you think."

"Invisible ink," muttered Chip. "Pamela, go to the cafeteria and get some hot chocolate. Bring it back to Mr. Gonshak's room."

"What am I? The secretary?" demanded Pamela.

"You wanted to help Invisible Inc.," said Justin. "Here's your chance."

Just then, Charlene's parents came down the hall.

"Philip, what are you doing here?" they asked.

"I came to hear Charlene read her story," said Philip, looking embarrassed.

"How sweet," said Charlene's mother.

Charlene glared at Philip.

"Mom, Dad, everybody, let me talk to Charlene alone, okay?" Philip asked. Then he and Charlene walked down the hall.

"I was jealous," Philip whispered to her.

"Jealous of me?" asked Charlene, shocked.

"Yes," admitted Philip. "I was so used to being the smartest one in the family. I'm sorry."

"Come on, everybody!" shouted Chip. "It's finally time to hear Charlene's story."

Charlene went over to Chip. "Are you sure my paper's okay?" she asked.

"Philip isn't as smart as he thinks he is," said Chip. "He didn't lie. He did proofread your paper. Then he copied it over in invisible ink."

Pamela came back with a steaming cup of hot chocolate. Justin and Chip held the blank piece of paper over the steam. Slowly, Charlene's words became visible.

* * *

Back in the classroom, Charlene stood in front of the group of parents and kids. She took a deep breath and began reading.

"My story is called:

Too Tough for Monsters

Once, two parents lived on a planet in a distant galaxy. They had three children, but the youngest was so little he didn't count."

"Wait a minute!" shouted Stanley. "I count."

"This is fiction," said Charlene. "When you get out of kindergarten, you'll find out the difference between fiction and nonfiction."

"I already know that," bragged Stanley.

"Charlene," said Mr. Gonshak with a small smile, "just go on with your story."

"One day, a monster came and threatened to eat the whole family. The oldest boy was very smart. He knew that the sister was a little bossy, and some people thought she was tough. He told the monster to eat his sister because she was so tough.

'She'll be okay,' he told his mother. 'She's so tough the monster will spit her out.'

But the little girl wasn't as tough as she looked. Just as the monster was about to eat her, she started to cry. Her tears melted the monster, and it turned into a big puddle. They all had to swim for their lives. The smart brother never learned how to swim. But his sister was one of the world's greatest swimmers. She saved her brother."

Charlene looked up.

"*Even though he had been mean,*" she added, although that hadn't been in her original story.

"What happened to the littlest brother?" demanded Stanley.

"He lived happily ever after," said Charlene.

"What happened to the older brother?" asked Pamela.

"He learned not to try to fool Invisible Inc.," said Philip from the back of the room.

Everybody in the room laughed, but nobody laughed harder than Charlene, Justin, and Chip.